D0487644

A catalogue record for this book is available from
the British Library

This edition published 1992
by BCA by arrangement with Ladybird Books Ltd

Printed in England (7)

CN 6656

BCA
LONDON · NEW YORK · SYDNEY · TORONTO

Chapter One

Once upon a time there lived a handsome young prince. His home was a magnificent castle and his clothes were the finest that money could buy.

But although he had grown up with everything anyone could want, the Prince was selfish, spoiled and unkind. Since he was the Prince, no one ever said no to him. And no one ever even thought of teaching him a lesson.

Until one bitterly cold winter's night when an old beggar woman came to the castle. She was shivering and weak, and the servants took pity on her. They led her to the Prince. She bowed to him, taking a red rose from her basket.

"Kind sir," she said, "would you grant me shelter from the cold? I have no money, but I can offer you this small, perfect rose as a token of my gratitude."

The servants had been sorry for the poor woman, but the Prince saw only her dirty rags and ugly face. "Go away," he said. "And keep away from my mirrors on the way out, in case they crack in horror at the sight of you!"

The woman looked back at him, unafraid. "My lord," she said, "do not be deceived by my rags. True beauty is found within."

The Prince wasn't listening. "Throw this ugly old bag of bones out of my castle," he ordered his servants. But before the servants could touch her, a powerful light began to glow all round her. As they looked on in awe, the old woman grew tall and beautiful. Now she was an enchantress, and her eyes shone bright with anger.

The Prince fell to his knees, trembling with fear. "Please forgive me," he cried. "I... I didn't know –"

The Enchantress ignored his pleading. "There is no love in your heart for anyone or anything," she said. "That makes you no better than a beast – and so you shall *become* a beast!"

The Prince shrank back in horror. "Please... no," he begged.

But the Enchantress showed no mercy. She raised her hands high, and slowly the young Prince changed. Dark hair sprouted on his face and hands, and claws grew from his fingertips. His teeth became long and sharp.

"I am casting a spell on the entire castle," the Enchantress said in a terrible voice. "You shall be a prisoner here – with no human company."

And at that moment, everyone else in the castle changed too. They changed into furniture, china, even knives and forks, until not one human being was left. The head of the household, Cogsworth, became a mantel clock, and the butler, Lumiere, became a candelabra. The cook, Mrs Potts, turned into a teapot. The castle became still and silent.

Then the Enchantress held up the rose she had brought. "This rose will bloom until your twenty-first birthday, and then it will wither and die. If you don't break the spell before the last petal falls, you will be doomed to remain a beast for ever."

"But how *can* I break the spell?" asked the frightened Beast. His voice was now a raspy snarl.

"There is only one way," said the Enchantress. "You must love another person, and earn that person's love in return."

She put the rose under a glass jar on a table, then showed him a small silver mirror. "I shall also leave you a gift. This enchanted mirror will show you any part of the world you wish to see. Look well, for it is a world you no longer belong to!"

Then there was a flash of light, so bright that the Beast hid his eyes. When he opened them, the Enchantress had disappeared.

He left the room and ran up the stairs of the castle tower. Up, up, up he climbed, tripping over his new, clumsy, hairy feet. When at last he reached the top, he gazed down from the tower window.

He was shocked by what he saw. There was not one person in the castle grounds, not one house, not one road, not one grassy field. The sunny countryside had been swallowed up by a thick grey mist.

The Enchantress had said he would have to earn another person's love. But where was he to find someone? "And even if I do find someone, who could ever learn to love a beast?" he thought.

He threw back his head and howled in despair. He had lost everything.

Chapter Two

Not far from where the castle now lay hidden beneath the mist was a charming little village. And in that village lived a girl more beautiful than any other girl in the land. Her name was Belle.

She was so lovely that when she walked through the tiny village, everyone turned to look at her. The baker, the blacksmith, the fruitseller, the milkmaid – even the children would stop what they were doing to watch her go by.

But Belle never noticed their glances. She was always too busy reading. She even read as she walked along.

"She's so pretty," the villagers would say, shaking their heads. "What a pity she always has her head buried in a book. She's just as strange as her father."

To Belle, there was nothing strange about reading. In books she could find magic, romance and excitement. There were adventures and Prince Charmings and happy endings. Books were much more interesting than her quiet village, where every day was the same as the one before.

She loved going into the bookshop, where the kindly owner would often lend her a book to read. Sometimes when there were no new ones, she would get an old favourite to read once more.

As for her father, Maurice, Belle was very proud of him. To her, he didn't seem strange at all. She thought he was the cleverest inventor in the whole world.

True, Maurice was a bit forgetful. True, his inventions never seemed to work quite the way they were supposed to. But Belle knew that one day he would succeed. And when he did, she was sure he would take her somewhere glamorous and exciting where she could meet her own Prince Charming. Till then, she would have to wait – and read – and fight off the foolish men who wanted to marry her.

Like Gaston. Gaston was a fine handsome hunter, admired by many of the young women of the village. But he was also a coward and a cheat. And he was always boasting.

One autumn day, as Belle walked through the marketplace, reading, Gaston said to his friend Lefou, "There she is, Lefou. That's the lucky girl I'm going to marry."

"The inventor's daughter?" said Lefou, surprised. "The one who always has her nose in a book? She's strange. She's..."

"The most beautiful girl in town," said Gaston quickly. "And don't I deserve the best?"

"W-why, yes, of course," stuttered Lefou. "But..."

Gaston ran after Belle, with Lefou following close behind. "Hello, Belle!" he said with a conceited smile.

Belle glanced up. "Oh, hello, Gaston," she answered, turning back to her book.

Gaston snatched the book out of her hand and flicked through it. Smiling down at her, he said, "How can you read this? It doesn't even have pictures. Anyway, it's not right for a girl to read. It's about time you got your head out of all these books, Belle, and paid attention to more important things – like me."

"Gaston, may I have my book back please?" said Belle, trying to be patient.

Gaston grinned. He tossed her book into a puddle, then he took her arm. "Come on, Belle, let's walk over to the tavern to look at my hunting trophies."

Belle pulled away from him, furious that he had ruined her book. "Sorry, I can't. I have to get home to help my father. Goodbye!" She picked up her book and began to walk away.

Lefou muttered to Gaston, "That crazy old man certainly needs all the help he can get."

Belle heard, and turned on him. "Don't talk about my father that way. He's not crazy. He's a genius!"

But before she could say anything else – BOOOOOOM! – an explosion shook the ground.

A plume of smoke rose from a small house just up the road. Belle's house!

"Papa!" screamed Belle. She ran home as fast as she could.

When she pulled open the door of her father's workshop, thick smoke billowed out. In the midst of it, sitting beside a heap of broken wood and metal gears, was her father, Maurice.

She ran to his side. "Are you all right, Papa?"

Coughing, Maurice stood up and kicked his invention. "How on earth did that happen? I'll never get this stupid contraption to work!" he muttered.

Belle smiled, relieved that he wasn't hurt. "Oh yes, you will," she said. "And you'll win first prize at the fair tomorrow – *and* become a world famous inventor."

Her father looked at her. "You really believe that?" he asked, a small smile flickering across his face.

"I always have," said Belle confidently.

"Well, then, what are we waiting for?" Maurice said, grabbing one of his tools. "I'll have this thing fixed in no time."

Belle watched him, thinking. Gaston's mocking words came back to her. *It's not right for a girl to read.*

"Papa," she said, "do you think I'm odd?"

Maurice popped out from behind his invention, his glasses crooked, his hair standing on end. "Odd? Now where did you get that idea?" he asked, puzzled.

"I don't know, I'm just not sure I fit in here," said Belle sadly. "Oh, Papa, I want excitement and adventure in my life... and I want someone to share it with," she added softly.

"What about Gaston?" said Maurice. "He's a handsome fellow. Don't you like him?"

"Oh, he's handsome enough. But he's not for me," said Belle. "He's rude and conceited."

"Well, don't you worry. This invention's going to be the start of a new life for us." Maurice gave his daughter a warm smile. "Then you can have a chance at those dreams."

Before long, he had the machine working again. There was plenty of time left to take it to the fair, and Belle helped him to load it onto a wooden wagon. Then they hitched the wagon to their family horse, Philippe. Maurice drew a cape round his shoulders, mounted the horse and rode off.

"Goodbye!" shouted Belle, waving after him. "Good luck!"

* * *

As Philippe trotted down the road, Maurice peered at a map, trying to make sure he was going the right way. It wasn't until it began to get dark, three hours later, that he suddenly realised that the map was upside down.

Maurice groaned. He was lost! "Now we'll never get to the fair in time," he said. "Belle will be so disappointed."

When they came to a fork in the road, there was a signpost, but the letters on it had faded away a long time ago.

To the left, the road went along a river. To the right, it disappeared into a thick, misty forest. Maurice peered up both roads, then pulled the reins to the right. "Let's go this way," he said.

But Philippe stopped dead and shook his head. Maurice just pulled harder. "Come on, Philippe. It's a shortcut. We'll be there in no time."

So they went to the right, into the forest. The road grew narrower, and trees cast black shadows on the ground. A thick grey fog began to settle over them. The drip, drip, drip of water falling from a branch echoed in the silence.

Then a sharp wind blew up, making the branches jerk like bony fingers. Maurice held his cloak closed against the cold and Philippe's ears twitched at every sound.

Suddenly a long shadow slipped through the trees. Philippe stopped once more. He looked round fearfully.

"Perhaps we'd better turn back..." Maurice began.

But it was too late. A pair of pale yellow eyes appeared in the bushes. Philippe whinnied, rearing up on his hind legs.

Maurice couldn't hold on, and he tumbled to the ground as Philippe galloped away.

He got to his feet and peered into the darkness. He whispered, "Philippe?" but the horse had gone.

Maurice saw the yellow eyes again, and hoped against hope that they belonged to something friendly.

But there was nothing friendly about the creature that appeared out of the darkness. It was a wolf!

Chapter Three

Grrrrrrrrrrr...

The wolf growled softly in its throat as Maurice gazed through the mist. For a moment he couldn't move, then he began to back away, slowly.

The wolf sprang towards him, and Maurice turned and ran. As he crashed through the bushes, he could hear the wolf padding after him. He glanced back to see another shadow, and another. It was a whole pack of wolves, panting and snarling. Maurice ran left, then right, but it was no use. The next time he looked back, many pairs of eyes were gaining on him.

And that was when a dim, far-off light caught his eye. He raced towards it, his heart leaping with hope. But the trees became thicker. Thorns ripped at him, and branches seemed to push him back like arms. The wolves were hard on his heels.

Then Maurice smacked against something hard. Metallic. A gate! "Help!" he cried. "Is someone there? Help!"

He pushed hard. The gate creaked open, and Maurice raced through. He slammed the gate shut just seconds before the wolves hurled themselves against it.

Maurice heaved a sigh of relief. At least he was safe for a little while. He turned round to see an enormous castle towering above him. A dark, old, crumbling castle surrounded by thick grey mist.

Maurice crossed a bridge over a dried-up moat and found himself in the castle grounds. Weeds and vines crept up garden walls and tangled round broken marble statues.

Although it looked as though no one had lived there for many years, the light that shone from the castle meant that *someone* must be inside.

Just then a flash of lightning split the sky, casting a harsh white light over everything, and rain began to fall in torrents.

Maurice ran across the bridge leading to the entrance of the castle and knocked on the door. When there was no reply, he cautiously pushed open the door and stepped inside.

On a table near the door stood a beautiful, lighted candelabra and a mantel clock. Round the walls hung rich tapestries and ornate paintings. Magnificent statues stood in corners, and the floors were covered with thick carpets. Archways in the distance led to dark, faraway rooms.

Staring with wonder, Maurice managed to call out, "Hello?"

Maurice's voice echoed as he fell silent again. Then he called out once more: "Hello? I don't mean to intrude, but I've lost my horse and I need a place to stay for the night."

A moment passed, then suddenly Maurice heard voices. The first whispered, "The poor fellow must have lost his way in the woods, Cogsworth."

The second whispered back, "If we keep quiet, Lumiere, maybe he'll go away."

"Oh, Cogsworth, have a heart," came the first voice again. Then, louder, it said, "You are welcome here, monsieur!"

"Who said that?" asked Maurice. "Where are you?"

Maurice felt something tugging at his cloak. He whirled round but saw no one.

"Down here!" said the second voice.

When Maurice looked down, he couldn't believe his eyes. The mantel clock was tugging at him. It had arms and legs – and a face!

"You're... you're alive!" said Maurice, picking up Cogsworth and poking him. "How can that be?"

"Of course I'm alive!" said the clock angrily. "I am Monsieur Cogsworth, and if you don't put me down at once, sir, I shall have to give you a sound thrashing!"

Maurice quickly set Cogsworth down on the table again, saying, "I beg your pardon, it's just that – AAAAAAH-CHOO!" A sneeze exploded out of him.

"You are soaked to the bone, monsieur," said the candelabra in a kind voice. "I am Monsieur Lumiere, at your service. Now come and warm yourself by the fire."

"No!" Cogsworth snorted. "I forbid it! The Master will be furious if he finds him here!"

But Lumiere paid no attention. He led Maurice into a huge drawing room where a roaring fire gave off a warm, amber glow. Maurice settled himself in a comfortable leather armchair.

"No! Not in the Master's chair," cried Cogsworth, putting his hands over his eyes. "I can't believe I'm seeing this!"

24

A tea trolley rolled into the room. On it was a round teapot with a plump, friendly face, and a small, chipped teacup.

"I'm Mrs Potts and this is my son Chip," said the teapot. "Would you like a spot of tea, sir? It'll soon warm you up."

"No!" shouted Cogsworth. "No tea!"

"Yes, please," said Maurice gratefully.

As Mrs Potts poured tea, Cogsworth grabbed Lumiere. "We've got to get him out of here! You know what the Master will do if…"

"Calm yourself," said Lumiere. "The Master doesn't need to know."

"Shhh, both of you!" said Mrs Potts, nodding towards Maurice. He was falling into a deep, blissful sleep…

BANG! The door flew open and Maurice fell from his chair in a panic. The tea trolley quickly rolled away, and Cogsworth hid under a carpet.

Maurice gasped as he saw someone – some*thing* – standing in the doorway. It towered on thick, hairy legs, and its head and arms were covered with matted fur. The floor shook under its feet as it stepped towards Maurice and said in a low growl, "There's a stranger here."

Maurice wanted to run, but he was transfixed with fear.

Lumiere stepped forward quickly. "Master," he said, "allow me to explain. The gentleman was lost in the woods. He was cold and wet, so…"

"RRRRRAAAAGGGGGHHH!" The force of the Beast's roar blew out every one of Lumiere's candles.

Cogsworth peered out from under the carpet. "Master, I was against it from the start," he said. "I tried to…"

The Beast moved closer. "What are you staring at?" he demanded.

"N-n-nothing," Maurice stammered.

"You come into my home and stare at me!" the Beast accused him angrily.

Maurice bolted for the door, but the Beast blocked his way. "I meant no harm," said Maurice. "I just needed somewhere to stay."

The Beast grabbed Maurice with his powerful claws and said in a sinister voice, *"I'll give you a place to stay!"*

Maurice was sure his last hour had come. Would he ever see his daughter, Belle, again?

Chapter Four

Gaston and Lefou walked proudly down the road to Belle's house, dressed in their finest clothes. Behind them came a priest and a brass band, as well as nearly everyone who lived in the village.

When they arrived at the house, Gaston turned to make a speech. "Ladies and gentlemen, I'd like to thank you all for coming to my wedding! But first," he said, chuckling, "I'd better go in there and propose to the girl!"

The crowd looked at one another and laughed. Gaston marched up to Belle's door and knocked hard.

Inside, Belle was reading. She put down her book, went to the door and opened it a little way. "Gaston, what a pleasant surprise," she said as politely as she could.

Gaston pushed past her into the house. "Belle," he announced, "there's not a girl in the village who wouldn't love to be in your shoes. This is the day your dreams come true!"

"What do *you* know about my dreams?" asked Belle.

Gaston sat down on her chair and put his feet up on the table. His muddy boots were right on top of her book.

"Imagine a hunting lodge in the heart of the country," he said. "My latest kill is roasting on the fire, and my little wife is getting the dinner ready. The little ones – we'll have six or seven of them – are playing on the floor. And do you know who that little wife is going to be? You, Belle!"

Belle's mouth fell open in disbelief. He was proposing to her – and he had invited the whole village to watch! What a cheek!

He stood up and tried to throw his arms round Belle. But she backed away towards the door, thinking fast. "Gaston, I'm... I'm... speechless! I don't know what to say!"

Gaston followed her round the room, finally catching her with her back to the door. "Say you'll marry me!"

"I'm really sorry, Gaston," said Belle, feeling behind her for the doorknob, "but I... I just don't deserve you. Thank you for asking me, though."

At last she found the doorknob. She turned it and pushed. Then, as the door opened, she moved aside. Gaston tumbled straight out into a puddle, and Belle slammed the door shut.

The crowd fell silent. Lefou walked slowly up to Gaston. "Turned you down, did she?" he asked.

Gaston got up with his fists clenched and his eyes burning with anger. Nervously, people began to back away.

Then suddenly, he burst out laughing. "Turn me down? Nonsense! She's just playing hard to get!" And with a smile fixed on his face and his head held high, he strode back to town.

No one saw his smile quickly turn to a scowl of anger. And no one heard his solemn vow: "I'm going to have Belle for my wife. One way or another."

* * *

Belle stayed in her house until every single person had left. When at last she opened the door, she heard a familiar noise – Philippe's whinny.

"Papa?" she thought. "Back so soon?"

But when she looked up the road, she saw Philippe was alone. She ran towards him, crying out, "Philippe! What's happened? Where's Papa?"

Philippe snorted and whinnied anxiously.

Belle was really worried. "We have to find him! Take me to him!"

She unhitched the wagon, then leapt on Philippe. He galloped down the road until they came to the forest. It was just as dark and creepy as before, but this time Philippe was determined to be brave. The wind howled and whistled all round them, but he trudged onwards.

Belle was terrified. She had never seen such a horrible place, even in her worst nightmares.

Philippe came to the rusty iron gate and stopped. Belle got down and pulled him towards it. And as soon as she pushed it open, she saw a hat lying on the ground. It was her father's!

"Papa!" she cried. "Come on, Philippe!" She dragged him into the castle grounds and tied him to a post. Then she ran into the great hall.

"Papa?" she called out as she went in. She ran through the hall and up a curved marble staircase. "Papa, are you here? It's Belle!"

When she reached the top of the stairs, Belle ran down a corridor – right past Cogsworth and Lumiere.

Cogsworth was frozen with surprise, but Lumiere nearly exploded with joy. "A girl!" he cried. "And such a beautiful one! After all these years, she's come to fall in love with the Master and break the spell!"

"Nonsense!" snapped Cogsworth. "She's come to find that poor fellow locked in the tower. He must be her father."

"Then we must help her!" said Lumiere. He took a shortcut to get ahead of Belle, and stopped in the corridor that led to the tower stairs.

When Belle reached the stairs, she saw Lumiere's flickering light. She called out, "Hello? Is someone there? I'm looking for..."

Lumiere moved up the stairs, then sat on a small shelf. Belle quickly followed him. When she got to the top she looked round, puzzled. All she could see was a candelabra and a row of doors with small grilles at the bottom. "That's funny," she said. "I'm sure there was someone..."

Then a hoarse voice said, "Belle?"

She knew at once who it was. "Papa!" she called. "Where are you?"

Maurice's face peered out from a grille in one of the doors. "Here I am." He put his hand out through the bars.

Belle ran to the door. "Oh, Papa, your poor hands are like ice," she said, as she took his hand in hers. "We must get you out of there!"

Shivering, Maurice said, "I don't know how you found me, Belle, but I want you to leave at once. You must go now!"

"No, Papa, I won't leave you!" vowed Belle.

Suddenly she felt darkness settling over her. At first she thought the candelabra had flickered out. But when she turned round, she realised the darkness was a shadow. The shadow of someone enormous, someone she couldn't see.

"Who's there?" she asked.

But the Beast couldn't answer her at once. He felt ashamed of his ugliness as he stared down at the most beautiful human being he had ever seen.

"Who are you?" Belle asked again, peering into the darkness.

Softly, the Beast said, "The Master of this castle."

"I've come for my father," Belle pleaded. "Please let him out! He's sick!"

"He shouldn't have come into my castle," replied the Beast.

Belle struggled to see his face. "Please, I'll do anything to save his life," she said. "Take me instead!"

Silence hung in the air. The Beast looked at Belle carefully. Her hair, her eyes, her lovely face, made him feel warm inside. It was the first time in years he had felt like that. "You would take his place?" he asked.

"Belle, no!" shouted her father. "You don't know what you're doing!"

Belle took no notice of him. "If I did take his place," she said, "would you let him go?"

"Yes," answered the Beast. "But you must promise to stay here for ever."

The corridor grew silent again. For ever? That made Belle think hard. Who was this man? Before she could give an answer, she would have to see him. "Come into the light," she said.

The Beast stood still, ashamed. But a desperate hope glimmered inside him. Perhaps, just perhaps, she wouldn't hate what she saw too much. She might even like him.

Slowly, he moved into the light.

Belle's eyes widened with horror. She gasped and turned away.

"No, Belle!" said Maurice. "I won't let you do this!"

But Belle was gathering her strength. She knew there was only one thing to be done, however dreadful it seemed.

She turned to face the Beast, her chin up. "You have my word."

"Done!" said the Beast. And without another word he unlocked the door and dragged Maurice out of the cell, down the corridor and out of the castle.

Maurice fought hard to get free, but he couldn't break the Beast's iron grip. "Please spare my daughter," he pleaded. "She had no part in this."

But the Beast didn't even hear him. As he pushed Maurice out of the castle grounds, there was only one thought on his mind.

The girl was his. For ever.

Chapter Five

Now that Belle was locked in the tower, the Beast had no idea what to do. He paced back and forth beneath the tower stairs muttering, "After all these years... after I'd given up hope... what do I say to her?"

Lumiere watched him. He wanted so much for the Beast to do the right thing. Perhaps – just perhaps – the Beast could make Belle fall in love with him. And if he did, the spell would be broken at last.

It was the only hope for Lumiere, and for all the other servants, to become human again.

Gathering up his courage, Lumiere said, "Er, Master... I was just thinking... since the girl is going to be with us for quite some time, perhaps you should offer her a more comfortable room."

The Beast growled, and Lumiere backed away in fright.

Then, muttering again, the Beast began to climb the tower stairs. He shuffled down the corridor to the cell and paused. Now it was *his* turn to gather up courage.

When the Beast opened the door, Belle was sitting on the ground, her head in her hands. She looked up at him tearfully. "I'll never see him again – and you didn't even let me say goodbye!"

The Beast frowned. He couldn't understand why Belle was unhappy, and he wasn't sure what he ought to do. "I'll show you to your room," he growled at last. He quickly walked back into the corridor, snatching up Lumiere in his thick paw on the way.

"My room?" Belle was confused. She had thought the Beast would be keeping her in the tower. She followed him down the stairs and through a long maze of corridors. They were both so silent that Lumiere could stand it no longer.

"*Say* something to her," he whispered to the Beast.

The Beast was so nervous he felt butterflies in his stomach. "I... hope you'll like it here," he said to Belle at last, then looked at Lumiere for approval.

Lumiere smiled. "Go on," he encouraged him.

"The castle is your home now, so you can go anywhere you like," said the Beast, "except the West Wing."

"What's in..." Belle began to ask.

Before she could finish, the Beast turned on her angrily. "It's forbidden!"

Lumiere groaned. The Beast wasn't helping himself at all.

Silence fell once more until they reached a large guest room. The Beast opened the door, and Belle walked in.

"If you need anything, my servants will look after you," said the Beast.

"Invite her to dinner!" Lumiere whispered to him.

"Oh." The Beast nodded, then turned back to Belle. "You'll... er... join me for dinner."

Belle wanted nothing more to do with him. Without answering, she pushed the door closed.

But the Beast stopped the door with his huge paw and said in a threatening voice, "That's not a request!"

Belle shut the door in his face, and the Beast snarled and stomped away.

Lumiere sighed heavily. If this was going to be a love affair, it certainly wasn't getting off to a good start.

* * *

Back in the village, in a noisy, crowded tavern, Gaston was brooding over Belle. "Who does she think she is, saying no to me?" he moaned into his beer. "I'm disgraced!"

"You?" said Lefou, bringing Gaston another drink. "Never! Why, everyone knows you're the strongest, the handsomest, the most *perfect* man in town!"

Gaston cheered up instantly. And in another instant, he was back to doing what he did best of all: boasting. He boasted about his hunting, his eating, his drinking, his fighting. He only stopped boasting when the tavern door opened with a loud THWACK!

Everyone fell silent and watched as a dirty, wet man stumbled in from the snow. At first no one recognised him.

"Help!" he cried, his face pale with terror. "Please help! He's got her! He's got Belle locked up in his castle!"

"It's crazy old Maurice!" yelled one of Gaston's friends. Laughter filled the tavern.

Gaston grinned up at Maurice from his chair. "What's all this about, Maurice? Just *who* has got Belle locked up?"

"A horrible, monstrous beast!" Maurice replied. "Please, please help me to rescue her!"

"All right, old man," said Gaston. "We'll help you out." He winked at his friends and pointed to the door.

Two of the men lifted Maurice up by his arms, took him to the door and threw him outside. The tavern crowd hooted and jeered, but Gaston grew thoughtful. He drew Lefou aside and said softly, "Crazy or not, that old man has given me an idea. I think I know how to make Belle my bride!"

And with an evil smile, he began to whisper his plan.

*   *   *

Maurice ran through the village streets looking for someone – anyone – who could help. "Please help me!" he shouted to everyone he saw. "My daughter has been captured by a beast!"

Everyone ignored him. "Old Maurice has gone completely crazy at last," they thought as they walked away.

As the snow went on falling, Maurice sank to his knees with one last, desperate cry: "Will no one help me?"

But only the harsh, whistling wind answered him. Maurice knew that unless he went back to save her himself, his poor daughter was doomed.

Chapter Six

As the sound of the Beast's footsteps grew fainter, Belle threw herself down on the bed and sobbed. She would never see her father again, nor any of the things she loved. She was in prison, and there she would stay for ever. The Beast would never let her go. How she hated him!

"And I will never, never have dinner with him!" she vowed to herself. "Even if he is the only other living thing in the castle."

The bed was soft, with a beautiful silk cover. And everything in the room was truly splendid, from the large wardrobe near the bed and the lovely carved wooden bedside table, down to the luxurious plush carpet that covered the floor.

But to Belle, none of that mattered. No matter how beautiful it was, the room was still a prison.

Then she heard a quiet knock on the door. "Who is it?" she asked.

"Mrs Potts, dear," came the answer. "I thought you might like some tea."

So there *were* some other people in the castle. Since the voice sounded warm and friendly, Belle opened the door.

There was no one there, only a round little teapot. But suddenly the teapot toddled happily into the room, with a little chipped teacup skipping along behind.

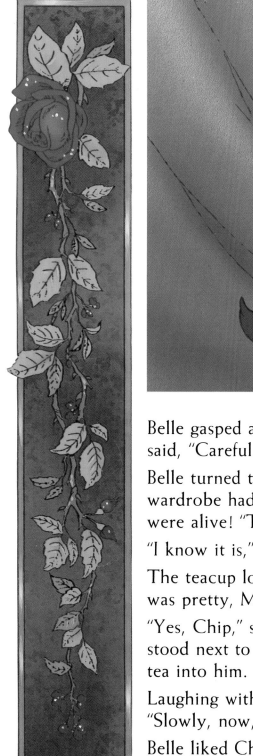

Belle gasped and backed away – right into the wardrobe, who said, "Careful!"

Belle turned to see who had spoken, and gasped again. The wardrobe had a face, just as the teapot and cup did. They were alive! "This... this is impossible!" cried Belle.

"I know it is," said the wardrobe, "but here we are!"

The teacup looked up at the teapot and said, "I told you she was pretty, Mama. Didn't I?"

"Yes, Chip," said Mrs Potts, smiling. "Now stand still." Chip stood next to her obediently, and she carefully poured some tea into him.

Laughing with excitement, Chip hopped over to Belle. "Slowly, now," Mrs Potts called. "Don't spill any!"

Belle liked Chip. "Thank you," she said, picking him up and taking a sip.

"That tickles!" said Chip with a giggle.

Mrs Potts looked at Belle and said, "You know, my dear, changing places with your father was a very brave thing to do."

"We all think so," agreed the wardrobe, sitting down next to Belle on the bed.

Belle looked down at the floor, her face unhappy. "But now I've lost my father, my dreams – everything!"

"It'll turn out all right in the end, you'll see," Mrs Potts said gently. Then, turning to Chip, she added, "Come along! I almost forgot we've got to get supper ready!"

As Mrs Potts and Chip hurried away, the wardrobe pulled a long, silky gown from one of her drawers. "Ah, you'll look lovely in this at dinner," she said.

"That's very kind of you, but I'm not going to dinner," Belle answered.

"Oh, but you must!" insisted the wardrobe, looking worried.

At that moment, Cogsworth appeared in the doorway. "Ahem!" he said, clearing his throat. "Dinner is served!"

But Belle had absolutely no intention of having dinner with the Beast. No matter who asked her, the answer was no!

*　*　*

Outside the dining room windows, snow was falling. The table was set with the finest china. Mrs Potts had come out of the kitchen to try and calm the Beast down, and she sat with Lumiere on the mantelpiece above a roaring fire. They watched the Beast pacing back and forth.

"What's taking her so long?" he growled.

"Do try to be patient, sir," said Mrs Potts.

"Master," added Lumiere, "have you thought that perhaps this girl could be the one to break the spell?"

"Of course I have!" the Beast roared. "I'm not a fool! But it's no use. She's so beautiful and I'm... well, look at me!"

The other two looked at each other. They knew what he meant.

"You must help her to see past all that," Mrs Potts said.

"I don't know how," the Beast replied sadly.

"Well, you can start by making yourself more presentable," said Mrs Potts. "Straighten up and try to act like a gentleman."

"Give her a dashing smile," suggested Lumiere. "Shower her with compliments."

"But be gentle," said Mrs Potts. "And sincere."

Then they both spoke at the same time. "Above all, you *must* control your temper!"

KNOCK! KNOCK! KNOCK!

Someone was at the door. "Here she is!" cried Lumiere. The Beast ran a paw through his hair and tried hard to smile. The door flew open.

But it was only Cogsworth.

"Well, where is she?" demanded the Beast.

"Er… who?" said Cogsworth nervously. "Oh, yes, you mean the girl. Well…"

The Beast glared at him impatiently, and Cogsworth knew there was no way out. He had to tell the truth. "She's not coming," he said, his voice a frightened squeak.

"RRRRRRRRAAAGGGGHHHH!" roared the Beast, bolting out of the room. He bounded up the stairs to Belle's room, with Lumiere, Cogsworth and Mrs Potts running behind.

"Your Lordship, let's not be hasty!" panted Cogsworth.

But the Beast wasn't listening. "You come out or I'll break the door down!" he bellowed, banging at Belle's door.

"I'm not hungry!" Belle shouted back.

"Master," Cogsworth said carefully, "*please* try to behave like a gentleman."

The Beast's eyes flashed with anger, but he knew Cogsworth was right. "It would give me great pleasure if you would join me for dinner," he said, grinding his teeth.

"No, thank you," Belle shot back.

That was more than enough for the Beast. "Fine!" he yelled. "Then you can go ahead and starve!" He whirled round to face Cogsworth and Lumiere. "If she won't eat with me, then she won't eat at all!" he roared.

Cogsworth threw up his hands and sighed. "We might as well go downstairs and start clearing up. Lumiere, stay and watch and let me know if there's the slightest change."

"My eyes will never leave that door," replied Lumiere.

* * *

The Beast strode angrily along the corridors to his lair in the West Wing. He threw his door open and stamped into the

room, muttering to himself, "I did ask nicely, but she refused! What am I supposed to do, beg?"

He picked up the magic mirror and demanded, "Show me the girl!"

The mirror shimmered with light, and slowly a vision of Belle's room appeared. Belle was sitting on the bed, her arms crossed in anger. As the Beast watched, the wardrobe walked over to her and said, "The Master's really not so bad once you get to know him. Why don't you give him a chance?"

"He's ruined my life!" replied Belle. "I don't want to have anything to do with him at all!"

The Beast didn't want to hear any more. "I'll always be just a monster to her," he said to himself. "It's hopeless."

And as he spoke, a petal fell from the wilting rose on his table and fluttered slowly to the bottom of the jar. The pile of shrivelled petals was growing bigger every day.

Chapter Seven

Later that night, Belle began to feel hungry. She listened at the door for a moment, then opened it quietly to look out. There was no one guarding her at all!

She could hear giggles coming from somewhere, and when she looked to her left, she saw Lumiere flirting with a pretty feather duster.

She tiptoed down the hall, getting hungrier and hungrier. She hadn't wanted to eat dinner with the Beast, but that didn't mean she wanted to starve!

She could hear the clanking of pots and pans behind a door in the distance, and she walked towards the sound. She had found the kitchen!

Slowly she pushed the door open. Cogsworth was there, and so was Mrs Potts. There was a stove there as well, angrily complaining about how his delicious food had gone to waste.

As soon as they saw Belle, everyone in the kitchen froze. Then Cogsworth broke the silence.

"Splendid to see you, mademoiselle," he said, with a deep bow. "I am Cogsworth, head of the household."

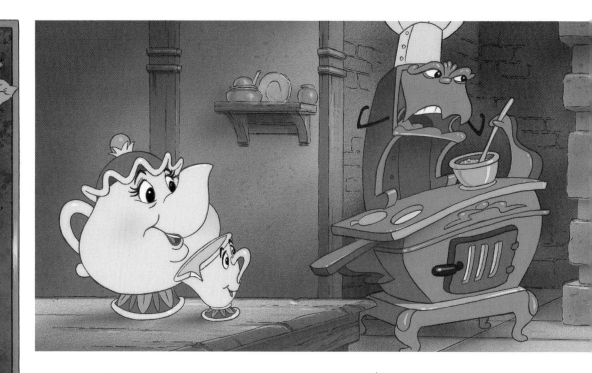

Lumiere burst in, out of breath and looking guilty. Glaring at him, Cogsworth said, "And this is Lumiere." He went on coldly, "If there's anything we can do to make your stay more comfortable…"

"I *am* a little hungry," Belle admitted.

Mrs Potts's eyes lit up. "You are?" she said. Turning to the others, she called out, "Hear that? Stoke the fire! Take out the knives and forks! Wake the china!"

"No!" shouted Cogsworth. "Remember what the Master said. If she doesn't eat with him, she doesn't eat at all!"

But no one listened. Instead, everyone and everything flew into action. The stove began cooking on all burners. Dishes full of good food leapt into the oven.

Smiling, Lumiere led Belle into the dining room. "Mademoiselle, it is with deep pride and great pleasure that we welcome you," he said grandly. "And now we invite you to relax and pull up a chair as the dining room proudly presents – your dinner!"

He behaved as if he were giving a show, and that was just what Belle saw: a show. She watched in wonder as the plates, dishes, and knives, forks and spoons all danced and sang on the table. Then a chair slid underneath Belle, and pushed her towards the table. The first course was served.

Every time the kitchen door swung open, Belle's mouth watered. And every plate of food was even more scrumptious than the one before.

The name of each dish was announced in song and dance. There were hot hors d'œuvres, beef ragout, cheese souffle, and a dessert of pie and flaming pudding. There was more food than Belle had ever seen before, but she managed to eat every morsel. She'd never had such a splendid dinner, nor seen such an unusual show! Even Cogsworth had at last entered into the spirit of things, dancing his heart out.

When it was all over, Belle clapped and cheered. "Bravo!" she cried. "That was wonderful!" Cogsworth, Lumiere and the others bowed deeply, grinning with pleasure.

"You know," Belle went on, "this is the first time I've ever been in an enchanted castle. Do you think I could have a look round?"

Cogsworth snapped out of his good mood in a flash. "Wait a second. I'm not sure that's a good idea. The Master..."

"Perhaps *you'd* like to take me," said Belle, smiling at him. "I'm sure *you* know everything there is to know about the castle."

"Well, yes," said Cogsworth, his chest swelling with pride. "As a matter of fact, I do."

So he took her on a tour of the castle. He talked and talked, explaining every single detail in every single room. Lumiere went with them, but he quickly became bored and paid less and less attention.

As they neared the West Wing, Cogsworth and Lumiere suddenly realised that Belle had disappeared. They looked everywhere, then Cogsworth spotted Belle moving up a dark set of stairs.

The two instantly raced ahead of her and blocked the way.

"What's up there?" she asked.

"Nothing!" Cogsworth replied. "Absolutely nothing of any interest in the West Wing. Dusty, dull, very boring."

"Ah, so this is the West Wing," said Belle, remembering the Beast's warning. "I wonder what he's hiding up there."

She started to take a step up, but Cogsworth didn't move. "Perhaps there's something else you'd like to see," he said desperately. "We have tapestries, gardens, a library..."

"A library?" said Belle, her interest caught.

"Oh, yes, indeed!" Cogsworth said. "We have a splendid library. With more books than you'll ever be able to read in a lifetime!"

He and Lumiere led her back downstairs. Cogsworth went on and on. "There are books on every subject, by every author who ever set pen to paper..."

The truth was that Belle did want to see the library, but for some reason she wanted to see the West Wing even more. She walked slower and slower, getting further and further behind the other two.

They were taking turns at describing the wonders of the library, and they didn't notice when Belle took two or three steps backward, then ran back to the West Wing stairs.

She raced up, two at a time. But when she got to the top, she stopped. Before her, a long, gloomy corridor stretched into darkness. Its walls were lined with mirrors, all of them broken. Slowly she walked past them into the deep shadows.

At the end of the corridor was an enormous wooden door. Above it, two hideous carved faces glared down at her. They seemed to be saying, "Stay away! Stay away!"

Belle took a deep breath. She pushed the door open and went in.

As she looked round, Belle's eyes widened, and a gasp caught in her throat. Every corner, every surface of the room was filthy. Vines grew in from an open window and twisted round broken furniture, cracked mirrors, and ripped paintings. Doors hung crookedly from torn hinges, and dirty sheets lay in a pile against one wall. Chewed bones were heaped in a corner.

As she walked further into the room, Belle shivered. "Surely this isn't where he lives?" she thought.

A painting on the wall drew her attention for a moment. It was a portrait of a young boy. Belle thought she had seen eyes like that somewhere before, but she couldn't think where. The painting had five deep slashes across it, as if the Beast had ripped it with his claws.

But then, in the midst of the dirt and the mess, Belle saw the rose. Although it was drooping and nearly all its petals had fallen off, it seemed to shimmer in the dim light. She went closer, reaching out her hand to the delicate petals.

Belle was so enchanted by the rose that she didn't notice the shadow of the Beast looming at the broken window.

59

Chapter Eight

"AAAARGGGGHHH!" the Beast roared as he leapt in front of Belle.

Belle screamed and backed away. Her fingers never touched the rose.

The Beast strode towards her, smashing everything in his way. "I warned you never to come here!" he shouted, hurling a heavy chair as if it were made of paper. "Don't you realise what could have happened?"

"I didn't mean any harm," pleaded Belle.

The Beast's only answer was to throw a table against the wall. "Get out!" he bellowed. "*Get out!*"

Belle wasted no time. She ran out of the room – and straight out of the castle. Promise or no promise, she was *not* going to stay there!

Philippe was waiting outside, right where she'd left him. Belle jumped on his back and shouted, "Take me home!"

Philippe's hooves thundered on the frozen earth. In seconds they were out of the castle grounds and into the woods. Belle began to feel happy once more.

But as soon as they plunged into the woods, the feeling left her. The forest was every bit as dark and thick as she remembered it. In the mist, Philippe couldn't see more than a few feet in front of him. But he could see the eyes – and so could Belle, the sinister yellow eyes of the wolf pack.

With angry growls, the wolves closed in on Philippe. He whinnied and reared onto his hind legs, and with a crash, Belle tumbled to the forest floor. It wasn't long before one wolf spotted her. Then another.

When they lunged at her, she scrambled away and grabbed a thick branch. She swung it at them, her heart racing with fear.

They danced round her, getting closer and closer. When she tried to back away, Belle tripped on a tangled root. Her ankle twisted under her, and she fell down.

This was the moment the wolves had been waiting for. They pounced. Belle felt their hot breath, and their claws on her neck. All hope left her, and she screamed.

Chapter Nine

Then, all of a sudden, someone pulled the wolves off Belle.

She could still hear them snarling behind her, only now they were attacking her rescuer! She turned and was startled when she saw who it was.

It was the Beast!

She stood up and ran to Philippe's side. Together they watched helplessly as the Beast fought the furious animals. The wolves slashed him with their teeth and claws, and he howled in pain.

But he was more than a match for them. He grabbed the wolves one by one and hurled them away. Those that were left saw that it was a losing battle. Whining, they turned tail and ran.

When at last the Beast stood alone, he tried to walk towards Belle. But after a few steps, he fell to the ground with a groan, his face twisted in agony.

Belle looked round. There was nothing to stop her escaping with Philippe. They were free to gallop back home, leaving the Beast and his horrible world behind.

The Beast lay on the ground in front of her, moaning in pain.

And Belle knew at that moment that she couldn't leave him there wounded in the snow, no matter how much she wanted to escape back to her own life.

"Help me to take him back, Philippe," she said softly.

She helped the Beast to his feet. Leaning against Philippe, he limped along, as they trudged back to the castle together.

In the grand hall, the Beast squirmed in pain as Belle dressed his wounds. "If you hadn't run away, this wouldn't have happened," he said angrily.

"If you hadn't frightened me, I wouldn't have run away!" replied Belle, cleaning one of his cuts with a wet cloth.

"Well, you shouldn't have been in the West Wing!" the Beast snapped.

"And *you* should learn to control your temper!" said Belle. They glared at each other for a long moment. Then their eyes dropped. Belle pulled her scarf off and began wrapping it round one of the wounds. "Hold still. This may hurt a little."

The Beast gritted his teeth and didn't move. Then, quietly, Belle said what she knew she should have said before. "By the way, thank you for saving my life."

"It was my pleasure," said the Beast with a smile. Pain or no pain, he suddenly felt very good inside.

* * *

At that same moment, Gaston and Lefou were walking towards Belle's cottage with a tall, skinny man with a sharp nose and small eyes. His name was Monsieur d'Arque, and he was the head of a lunatic asylum. He was going to play an important part in Gaston's evil plan.

For a bag of gold, he had agreed to throw Maurice into his asylum – unless Belle agreed to marry Gaston.

What none of them knew was that Maurice had left the cottage to rescue Belle, and was on his way into the woods. The cottage was empty.

"They have to come back some time," said Gaston. "Lefou, you stay here and keep watch."

While Lefou waited near the cottage, Gaston and Monsieur d'Arque walked back towards the village. Gaston was determined to find out where Maurice and Belle were. "No one is going to stop me from having Belle this time!" he said angrily.

*   *   *

Snow had fallen during the night. It covered the tangled vines and the broken statues, making the castle grounds look almost cheerful.

Since the evening of the wolf attack, the Beast was much more cheerful, too. And it was all because Belle had been so kind to him.

As he stood by his bedroom window, watching her walk along with Philippe, he thought to himself, "I would like to do something for her."

With the help of Cogsworth and Lumiere, he thought of a special gift for Belle. But it would take a lot of planning – and a lot of cleaning.

After hours of work, the gift was ready. The Beast led Belle down a hallway and stopped in front of a set of double doors. "I want to show you something," he said, "but first you have to close your eyes. It's a surprise."

Belle did as she was told. The Beast opened the door, then took her hand. He led her into a dark room with a high ceiling. "Can I open my eyes now?" she asked.

"Not yet," he said. Letting go of her hand, he went to a window and pulled back a curtain. Sunlight poured into the room.

"Now," said the Beast.

Belle opened her eyes, and they sparkled with delight. It was a beautiful library, filled with shelves and shelves of books. At one end, there was a roaring fire with a leather armchair in front of it.

"I can't believe it!" Belle said in awe. "I've never seen so many books in my life!"

The Beast smiled. "You like it? It's all yours," he said.

"Oh, thank you so much!" exclaimed Belle.

Hiding round a corner, Cogsworth and Lumiere looked happily at each other. Perhaps there was still a chance that the spell might be broken.

Over the next few days, things began to change between Belle and the Beast. To the delight of everyone in the household, they were becoming friends!

As Belle began to learn more about the Beast, she became his teacher as well as his friend. He didn't know how to eat with a knife and fork, so she taught him. He didn't know how to read, so she read to him. She taught him how to feed birds, and how to play in the snow.

"She doesn't shudder when she touches my paw any more," thought the Beast.

"There's something about him I didn't see before," Belle said to herself. "I thought he was ugly and cruel, but now he seems sweet and gentle."

For the first time in his life, the Beast was learning how to have fun. He was discovering new feelings inside himself, tender feelings he didn't know he could have. Feelings for Belle.

It wasn't long before the Beast realised that he was in love with Belle, and he knew he would have to do something about it.

He would have to tell her.

But how? How could he create a magical moment to sweep her off her feet? All at once he had an idea. He would invite Belle for a night of dancing in the ballroom!

He was delighted when she agreed. On the night of the dance, the Beast did something he had never done before. He bathed himself, dressed up, and even combed his mane.

As he walked to the ballroom stairs to wait for Belle, the Beast looked completely different. His mane shone in the light; his clothes were elegant. Lumiere provided romantic candlelight, and Mrs Potts sang a love song.

When Belle appeared at the top of the stairs in a shimmering gold gown, the Beast was stunned by her beauty. He was also very, very nervous.

He walked up the stairs, took her hand, and with a gallant smile he escorted her down. Then he whirled her onto the dance floor. He lifted his huge, hairy foot and took the first step – right onto Belle's toes.

The Beast was horrified. He'd gone to all this trouble to create a perfect evening and he'd spoiled it all. He was so clumsy.

But Belle didn't even frown. She gave him a warm smile and did what she had been doing for the last few days – she taught him.

The Beast slowly picked up the steps, and before long they were sweeping gracefully across the dance floor.

Soon, laughing and out of breath, they decided to go out on the balcony. As the Beast opened the door, cool air rushed in. The night was still, and the ground glimmered with snow in the moonlight. Above, thousands of stars twinkled in the night sky.

As she looked up, Belle sighed and smiled.

And the Beast knew that this was the moment to speak. "Belle," he said softly, "are you happy here... with me?"

Belle thought for a moment. She was certainly happier than she had expected to be. "Yes," she answered.

But the Beast could sense sadness in her eyes. "What is it?" he asked.

Belle looked at the Beast. She was close to tears. "If only I could see my father again. Just for a moment," she said. "I miss him so much."

The Beast gazed back at her for a long time. He knew now that he would do anything for her. "There is a way," he said.

Without another word, he led her into the West Wing and up to his room. There, he handed her the magic mirror. "This mirror will show you anything," he said. "Anything you wish to see."

Belle held it up. "I'd like to see my father, please," she whispered.

The mirror began to glow. An image appeared, dark and blurred. As it became clearer, Belle could see trees and bushes. It was the forest, and there was something moving through it. Something slow and hunched, like a wounded animal.

Then Belle recognised her father. He was calling, "Belle!" in a cracked, hoarse voice. Suddenly he fell to his knees, shaking and coughing.

"Papa!" screamed Belle. She turned to the Beast with panic in her eyes. "He's sick! He may be dying! And he's all alone!"

The Beast swallowed hard. As he looked at Belle's tear-streaked face and saw how unhappy she was, his heart skipped a beat. "Her father needs her now, but so do I," he thought.

The Beast glanced towards the table and saw two shrivelled petals clinging to the dying rose. Soon they would fall off. If he let Belle go now, he would never know if she loved him, and the spell would never be broken. He would remain a hideous Beast for all time.

But when he looked into Belle's eyes once more, he knew there was only one thing to do.

"You must go to him," he said, slowly speaking the words he knew would seal his doom for ever.

Belle stared at him in disbelief. "You mean, I'm free?" The Beast tried hard to keep his voice steady. "I release you. You're no longer my prisoner."

Belle gripped his hand joyfully. "Oh, thank you!" She began to hurry out of the door, but turned back when she realised she was still holding the magic mirror.

The Beast shook his head. "Take it with you," he said, "so that you'll always have a way to look back... and remember me."

Belle clutched the mirror to her chest. "Thank you for understanding how much he needs me," she said.

"I need you just as much!" were the words the Beast wanted to say.

But he didn't say them. Instead, he just nodded.

Belle touched his hand gently then ran out, her golden gown floating out behind her.

The Beast stood on his balcony to watch Belle as she left his castle. She mounted Philippe and galloped away, the moonlight glinting in her silken hair.

When they were gone, the Beast did something he hadn't done since he was a boy.

He threw back his head and howled from the pain in his heart.

Chapter Ten

"Thank goodness he's still alive!" was all Belle could think when she found her father in the snow. He was soaked to the skin, and he was feverish. He didn't even know who she was – but he was alive.

She managed to get him onto Philippe, and together they galloped at top speed through the snow-covered forest.

When they got to their cottage, Belle put Maurice to bed straightaway, and he fell into a long, deep sleep. She held his hand for hours, worried that he would never recover, never recognise her again.

When at last he woke up, he moaned, "It should have been me... me!" His eyes flickered and he gave Belle a blank stare. Then slowly, he smiled. "Belle?"

Belle was filled with relief. He knew who she was! "It's all right, Papa," she said. "I'm home."

Tears of joy filled Maurice's eyes, and he sat up and threw his arms round his daughter. They hugged and laughed and cried. "I missed you so much!" said Belle.

"But how did you escape the Beast?" asked Maurice.

"He let me go," Belle said softly.

Maurice was surprised. "That horrible Beast?"

"He's different now, Papa," Belle said with a sigh. "He's changed somehow."

Just at that moment, Belle thought she saw something moving in her saddlebag. She opened one of the flaps, and there was Chip, the teacup! He gave her a sheepish smile.

Belle smiled back. "Oh... a stowaway."

RAP! RAP! RAP! RAP!

Belle and Maurice were both startled by the loud knocking at the door. Belle covered Chip up again and went to open the door.

There stood a tall, thin man with a sharp nose and small eyes. Behind him was a wooden wagon with the words *Maison des Loons* on the side. A crowd of villagers, with Lefou in front, stood beside the wagon.

"May I... help you?" asked Belle, puzzled.

"I'm Monsieur d'Arque," said the man. "I've come to collect your father."

"He was raving like a lunatic outside the tavern!" Lefou added. "We all heard him, didn't we?"

Most of the crowd mumbled in agreement. Some men dressed in the white uniforms of the Maison des Loons stepped towards the house.

"My father's *not* crazy!" said Belle, standing firmly in the doorway. "I won't let you take him!"

Maurice came up behind Belle to see what was going on. As soon as Lefou saw him, he shouted, "Come on, Maurice, tell us again. How big *was* that beast?"

76

"Well, I'd say eight – no, more like ten feet tall!" Maurice answered seriously.

The crowd hooted with laughter. "You don't get much crazier than that!" shouted Lefou.

Forcing their way past Belle, Monsieur d'Arque's men grabbed Maurice and pulled him outside.

Maurice struggled in vain to free himself. "It's true, I tell you!" he shouted.

Belle ran after them. "You can't do this!" she cried.

Suddenly Gaston stepped out of the shadows and planted himself in front of Belle. With a calm smile he said, "Poor Belle. It's a shame about your father."

"You know he's not crazy!" snapped Belle, eyeing Gaston with suspicion.

"Hmmmm…" Gaston pretended to think hard. "I might be able to help, *if…*" his voice trailed off.

"If what?" asked Belle.

"If you marry me," Gaston answered.

Belle stepped back in shock. He was grinning at her, certain that his plan had worked. "One little word, Belle," he said. "That's all it takes."

"Never!" she said.

"Just as you like," said Gaston. He waved at Monsieur d'Arque's men. "Take him away."

Belle raced back into the house and brought out the enchanted mirror. "My father's not crazy," she shouted, "and I can prove it."

The crowd stared at her. Monsieur d'Arque's men stopped. Gaston looked up, worried.

Holding the mirror up for all to see, Belle said, "Show me the Beast!"

The mirror glowed, and the crowd gasped. Slowly the Beast's image appeared. He was pacing the balcony in torment. Then, throwing back his head, he let out a bloodcurdling howl.

People in the crowd screamed and ran away. Monsieur d'Arque's men leapt into their wagon and drove away, leaving Maurice behind. Someone shouted, "Is he dangerous?"

Belle looked tenderly at the Beast's image. "Oh, no. I know he looks vicious, but he's really kind and gentle."

Gaston was furious that his plan had failed. He grabbed the mirror and whirled round to the crowd. "She's as crazy as the old man!" he exclaimed. "The Beast will come after your children in the night! He'll wreck our village!"

Everyone began to panic, shouting angrily.

"No, he won't!" said Belle.

But Gaston went on, "We're not safe until his head is mounted on my wall! We must kill the Beast!"

When Belle tried to stop Gaston, he ordered his friends to grab her and Maurice. "We can't have them running off to warn the creature!" Gaston yelled to the frightened crowd. "Lock them in the cellar!" So Gaston's men forced Belle and Maurice down the cellar steps. As the door slammed shut over their heads, the last thing Belle saw was Gaston leading the crowd towards the forest.

They were shouting, "Kill the Beast! Kill the Beast!"

"But Master..." began Mrs Potts.

BOOOOOOOM! The sound of another battering-ram attack cut her off. "Kill the Beast! Kill the Beast!" came the chant of the crowd in the distance. "Kill the Beast!"

With a tremendous crash, the huge door fell in, and the objects behind it scattered.

But when Gaston's mob charged in, they stopped short. The great hall was empty. All they could see was a candelabra, a mantel clock and one or two other objects.

"Something fishy's going on around here," said Lefou, creeping closer and closer to Lumiere.

With a sudden jab, Lumiere poked him in the eye.

"YEOUCHHH!" screamed Lefou.

Lumiere bellowed, "CHAAAAARGE!" The battle was on.

Gaston's men couldn't believe their eyes. Candelabras, clocks, dishes, fire tongs, footstools, brushes – all fighting!

As his men fought, Gaston made his way further into the castle. He was going to find the Beast himself!

*   *   *

Meanwhile, outside the cottage, Maurice's invention stood on top of a gentle hill. It was a large contraption, a maze of ropes, levers, pulleys, wheels, bells and whistles. Chip, who had managed to sneak out of the house unnoticed, stared up at the amazing machine. He had absolutely no idea what it was or what it was supposed to do.

He walked round it once or twice, looking puzzled. Then he began to turn a few knobs and pull a few levers. Finally, he gave it a little nudge.

WHIR... CREAK... BLEEP...

The invention coughed to life! It began to roll forward, and Chip jumped up and down with glee. It rolled to the left, then to the right, then forward – straight towards the cellar door.

Maurice and Belle both heard a loud rumble. Maurice looked through the window in the cellar door and saw the contraption rolling towards them. "Belle, look out!" he shouted.

They threw themselves to one side just as Maurice's invention came bursting through the cellar door. On it, hanging from a small lever, was Chip.

"You did it, little teacup!" shouted Belle happily.

"Come on," said Maurice. As soon as they ran outside, Philippe saw them and whinnied joyfully.

"Philippe, my old friend," called Maurice. "Take us to the castle!"

*   *   *

In the castle, the battle raged on as Gaston's men stormed through room after room. Wherever they went, the objects rose up to defend their home.

Finally, Lefou and the others realised they were beaten and retreated. "And stay out!" shouted Cogsworth triumphantly.

But Gaston himself was in a quieter place. He was upstairs, just outside the Beast's lair. He pulled an arrow from his quiver. Then, lashing out with his foot, he kicked the door open.

The Beast was standing by the window, and he turned slowly to face Gaston. He didn't care what happened. Life meant nothing to him without Belle.

Gaston's arrow sliced through the air and landed firmly in the Beast's shoulder.

The Beast howled in agony and fell to the floor. As he struggled to stand up, Gaston came up behind him and kicked him. The Beast crawled out onto the balcony. With another howl of pain, the Beast tumbled over the balcony railing and landed on the smooth sloping slates of the castle roof.

Gaston grabbed a club that hung on the wall and went after the Beast. "Get up!" he shouted.

The Beast tried, but only got as far as his knees. Rain had begun to fall, and the roof was wet and slippery.

Climbing out onto the roof, Gaston swung the club above his head. With one mighty blow, he brought it down on the Beast's back.

The Beast howled again and collapsed. As he slid slowly down the side of the roof, Gaston said once more, "Get up!"

Gaston hit him again and again, and the Beast grew too weak to rise. Soon it would be all over.

"NOOOOOOOO!" a scream rang out from below.

With his last ounce of strength, the Beast turned his head. The voice was familiar, and it brought him back to life in an instant. Could it be?

Yes! It was Belle. She was racing towards the castle on her horse, and her father was with her.

Gaston knew it was Belle as well. Glaring at the back of the Beast's head, he shrieked "YEEEAAAHH!" at the top of his voice. Then he brought the club down as hard as he could.

Chapter Twelve

The Beast had no time to think. He turned to see Gaston's club coming towards him at lightning speed. The Beast's hand darted out, smacked into the side of the club, and stopped it in midair.

Gaston backed away as the Beast slowly rose to his full height and moved forward, fury in his face. His shadow seemed to swallow Gaston. Now, each time he tried to use his club, the Beast blocked it.

Roaring with rage, the Beast stalked after him. With a swipe of his long arm, he sent the club flying.

Suddenly there was a clatter of hooves on the castle stairs. Philippe had galloped right into the castle!

But the Beast hardly heard it. He was burning with anger – and he wanted revenge!

He lunged forward and grabbed Gaston by the neck. Then with a furious roar, he lifted him high into the air.

Gaston begged for mercy, but the Beast paid no attention. He held him over the edge of the roof, ready to send him tumbling to his death.

Then, suddenly, the Beast stopped.

It may have been the terror in Gaston's eyes, or Gaston's helplessness that stopped the Beast. Or it may have been that the time spent with Belle had simply made the Beast too human to kill.

Whatever the reason, he stood Gaston back on his feet and just said, "Get out."

Then he saw Belle. Her face was pale and her hair bedraggled from her wild ride. She was out of breath and looked exhausted.

But to the Beast she was beautiful. He began to limp towards her. She smiled warmly and held out her arms. Then suddenly she stiffened and a look of terror spread over her face. "Beast!" she screamed, pointing over his shoulder.

It was too late. Gaston was already lunging towards him, a
knife in his hand. Before the Beast could move, the knife was
deep in his back.

His roar of agony echoed into the night as he staggered
round to face Gaston.

The Beast's terrifying howl, and the look on his face, made
Gaston go white with fear. Trembling, he tried to back
away. Without looking, he took a hesitant step backwards,
only to get his foot caught in a gutter. As the Beast stumbled
forward, Gaston pulled his foot out – and lost his balance.
His arms whirling like a windmill, he fell, and slid to the
edge of the roof.

Then, in a flash, he was gone. His scream hung in the air as
he plunged over the side.

The Beast turned back and climbed slowly onto the balcony. He tried to stand up straight, but the effort was too much for him. Groaning, he collapsed.

Belle ran to him and knelt by his side. Tenderly, she cradled him in her arms.

His eyes smiled up at her. "You... came back," he said, gasping with pain. "At least... I got to see you one last time..."

Belle fought back her tears. She couldn't bear to see the Beast in pain. "Please don't talk like that," she said. "You're going to be all right."

At that moment Cogsworth, Lumiere and Mrs Potts rushed up to the balcony window. They froze with horror at the sight of their fallen Master.

Behind them, the rose's last petal wavered in the breeze.

"Perhaps it's better this way," said the Beast, his eyes closing.

"No! Please… please!" Belle cried out in anguish. Tears flowed down her cheeks and spilled onto the Beast's face. She held his limp, wounded body closer to her and kissed him tenderly. "I love you!" she cried.

And as she spoke, the last rose petal floated slowly down to the table.

Chapter Thirteen

For a long, long moment, all was quiet, except for the sound of Belle weeping.

Then suddenly the rain began to sparkle and shimmer with light, and the air began to glow.

The Beast opened his eyes, and a healing warmth flooded through his body. He looked at his hands. The hair was disappearing! There were long, strong fingers where just a moment before there had been a mangled paw. He gasped, then reached up to touch his face.

It was smooth! And his wounds were gone. He felt as healthy and strong as... as... He hardly even dared to think the words – as healthy and strong as a young prince.

Could it be, or was he dreaming?

One look at Belle's face was enough to give him the answer. She was staring at him as if she'd never seen him before.

The Prince rose to his feet. It all came back to him in a rush – how it felt to stand perfectly straight. How it felt to be human. He hadn't forgotten.

But he was different now. He was taller, older, stronger. And he was looking at the whole world differently. Not with greed, and anger, and spite, but with kindness, understanding – and love.

"Belle," he said gently. "It's me."

She looked at him, startled, not knowing what to believe. But there was something about his smile, and about his eyes – they were the eyes of the Beast. The Beast whom she loved.

With a radiant smile, Belle ran into his arms. And there on the balcony, as the sun peeped over the horizon, they shared a tender kiss.

That kiss seemed to bring new magic to the castle. In a swirl of light and colour, Cogsworth turned into a sturdy man with a moustache. Lumiere became a tall, dashing butler, and Mrs Potts turned into a plump, sweet-faced woman.

"The spell is broken!" said Cogsworth, his face breaking into a joyful smile.

The Prince grinned at his faithful servants. He turned for a moment from Belle and threw his arms around them. In the distance, he could hear shouts of joy. The objects, from the East Wing of the castle to the West Wing, were turning back into the people they had once been.

Memories flooded back to the Prince. Memories of a beautiful, shining castle with flags flying and people running about – working, laughing, singing. Lush green meadows and a moat of deep blue water.

The night was lifting – and so were the years of gloom. As the sun rose, the grey mist disappeared and the countryside burst into bloom.

All around the Prince was beauty, but none of it could match the love he saw in Belle's eyes.

In one last happy burst of magic, everyone in the castle was whisked into the ballroom. Musicians played, lights twinkled, and the floor shone like a mirror.

The Prince held out his hand, and Belle joined him for a dance. As they whirled round the room, Belle saw happiness in every corner. Mrs Potts was hugging her little teacups, who were all real, live children now. One of them had a broken tooth.

"Chip!" called out Belle, waving to him.

She whirled round again and saw her father, Maurice, looking at everything in awe. The wardrobe, now a lovely lady-in-waiting, came to his side. She winked at him and he blushed.

Belle laughed. For years, she had thought fairy tales belonged only in books. But as she looked up into the gentle, loving eyes of her new-found Prince, she knew that wasn't true. And she knew just what the ending to her real-life fairy tale was going to be.

She and her Prince were going to live happily ever after.